30

ID0613859

Grafton Books
A Division of the Collins Publishing Group
8 Grafton Street, London W1X 3LA

Published by Grafton Books 1986

A TEMPLAR BOOK
Devised and produced by Templar Publishing
Old King's Head Court, Dorking, Surrey RH4 1AR

Illustrations copyright © 1986 by Templar Publishing Ltd
Text copyright © 1986 by Deborah Savage

Savage, Deborah
    Big Mouth. — (The Adventures of Peregrine Piecrust; v.6)
    I. Title II. Forsey, Chris III. Series
    823'.914 [J] PZ7

ISBN 0-246-13005-9

All rights reserved. No part of this publication may be
reproduced, stored in a retrieval system, or transmitted in
any form or by any means, electronic, mechanical,
photocopying, recording or otherwise, without the prior
permission of the publishers.

Origination by Positive Colour Ltd, Maldon, Essex
Printed and bound in Great Britain by Purnell and Sons
(Book Production) Ltd, Paulton, Bristol. Member of BPCC plc

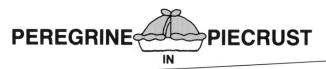

PEREGRINE PIECRUST

IN

BIG MOUTH

Written by Deborah Savage
Illustrated by Chris Forsey

GRAFTON BOOKS

A Division of the Collins Publishing Group

LONDON GLASGOW
TORONTO SYDNEY AUCKLAND

Peregrine Piecrust loved making a noise.

He liked nothing better than shouting at the top of his voice, or yelling and shrieking when everyone else wanted some peace and quiet.

"Go out and play in the garden!" said Mrs Piecrust, who had a headache.

Peregrine raced outside and pretended to be a fierce lion.

He tore round and round, roaring so loudly that all the birds flew away in fright. Even Tiddles the cat couldn't stand it. She clambered on to the garage roof and refused to come down until Peregrine had gone to bed.

At dinner that evening, Peregrine made so much noise that everyone had to stuff cotton wool in their ears.

Mr Piecrust even tried wearing headphones to deaden the sound of Peregrine's voice, and Baby Ben got so fed up that he threw his food all over the floor.

Peregrine didn't seem to notice. He just carried on shouting all the same.

Soon, everyone in Peregrine's street was talking about him … when they could hear themselves above his chatter, that is.

When Peregrine spoke, the people four doors away could hear him. Even the man who read the weather forecast on TV gave up because nobody could hear what he was saying. And Mrs Green from next door blamed Peregrine's noisiness for the fact that all her flowers were drooping.

Before long 'FOR SALE' notices had sprung up all along the street. But Peregrine didn't care.

As the days went by, Peregrine's voice got louder and louder. Now when he shrieked, walls cracked and windows shattered.

What's more, his mouth had started to get bigger. It stretched almost from one side of his face to the other and he could scarcely close it properly. Mrs Piecrust was worried that if it got any wider, the top of his head would fall off!

At school, Peregrine had to have all his lessons by himself because his classmates couldn't hear what Miss Prim was saying above the din.

But STILL Peregrine kept on shouting

Then one morning, Peregrine woke
up a little earlier than usual.
The house was very quiet so he
guessed that the rest of the family
were still asleep.

Peregrine stretched his arms.
He was just about to bellow
"Wakey, wakey!" to let them know
he was awake when...

SOMETHING DREADFUL HAPPENED!

Peregrine opened his mouth as wide as he could … but not a single sound came out. Not a squeak, not even a whisper.

Peregrine cleared his throat, took a deep breath and tried again.

Absolutely nothing happened! His voice had vanished.

Where had it gone?

Peregrine dashed out of bed and into his parent's room to find out.

Peregrine's parents were still asleep but he managed to wake up his father by jumping up and down on the bed. Then he opened his mouth and pointed excitedly down his throat.

It took the sleepy Mr Piecrust only a few seconds to grasp what had happened.

First he began to giggle. Then he began to laugh. And that woke Mrs Piecrust.

"Peregrine's lost his voice," Mr Piecrust chuckled to his wife. "Listen. It's so quiet you can even hear the birds singing!"

And Mrs Piecrust started laughing too.

Peregrine was furious.

Over breakfast, the Piecrusts discussed Peregrine's predicament (everyone except Peregrine, that is).

"You'll just have to keep quite quiet until you get your voice back again," laughed Mr Piecrust, smiling at his own joke.

"Where's Peregrine's voice gone?" asked Peregrine's sister Poppy.

"It's not GONE anywhere," said Mr Piecrust. "It's just that Peregrine's been making so much noise lately that he's strained his voice-box. Now it won't work properly until it's had a complete rest."

Poor Peregrine! What was he going to do?

Well, there wasn't much that Peregrine COULD do, except be quiet. His throat hurt, his jaws ached, and his lips went all frilly as his mouth gradually shrank back to its normal size.

His father made a sign for him to hang round his neck at school. It said "I HAVE LOST MY VOICE" in big letters. He also had to carry round a pen and paper, so that whenever a teacher asked him a question, he could jot down the answer. He became a very fast writer indeed.

All the people in Peregrine's street were delighted that the noise had stopped. The neighbours began to sit out in their gardens again and Mrs Green's flowers perked up no end!

The man who read the weather forecast was so grateful that he even sent Peregrine some flowers with a message to get well soon. But not TOO well and not TOO soon, he hoped.

Certainly not so well that he would start shouting again.

And after a long, quiet and very peaceful convalescence, Peregrine's voice returned to normal.

He wasn't nearly as noisy as before and had quite gone off the idea of shouting. In fact, he spoke so quietly that people often had to lean quite close to hear what he was saying.

Well, for a while, anyway...